To grandson Joshua Sidney Finchler, may your life be filled with as much joy as you have brought to ours. —J. F.

To Big Pat and the Vizzard Family. —K. O.

Text copyright © 2000 by Judy Finchler
Illustrations copyright © 2000 by Kevin O'Malley

First published in the United States of America in 2000
by Walker Books for Young Readers, an imprint of Bloomsbury Publishing, Inc.
www.bloomsbury.com

Bloomsbury is a registered trademark of Bloomsbury Publishing Plc

For information about permission to reproduce selections from this book, write to
Permissions, Bloomsbury Children's Books, 1385 Broadway, New York, New York 10018
Bloomsbury books may be purchased for business or promotional use. For information on bulk
purchases please contact Macmillan Corporate and Premium Sales Department at
specialmarkets@macmillan.com

The Library of Congress has cataloged the hardcover edition as follows:
Finchler, Judy.
Testing Miss Malarkey / Judy Finchler ; illustrations by Kevin O'Malley.
p.   cm.
Summary: Although the teachers, the principal, and parents say The Test is not important, their actions tell another story.
ISBN 0-8027-8737-1 (hardback) • ISBN 0-8027-8739-8 (reinforced)
[1. Achievement tests—Fiction. 2. Schools—Fiction.]
I. O'Malley, Kevin, ill. II. Title.
PZ7.F495666 Te 2000   [E]—dc21   00-028100

ISBN 978-0-8027-7624-2 (paperback)

Book design by Sophie Ye Chin
Printed in China by C&C Offset Printing Co., Ltd., Shenzhen, Guangdong
21 23 25 27 29 30 28 26 24 22 20

TESTING MISS MALARKEY

Judy Finchler
illustrated by **Kevin O'Malley**

BLOOMSBURY
NEW YORK   LONDON   OXFORD   NEW DELHI   SYDNEY

Miss Malarkey is a good teacher. Usually she's really nice. But a couple of weeks ago she started acting a little weird. She started talking about THE TEST: The Instructional Performance Through Understanding test. I think Miss Malarkey said it was called the "I.P.T.U." test.

But Miss Malarkey said THE TEST wasn't that important. She said it wouldn't affect our report cards. It wouldn't mean extra homework. And if we didn't do well, we'd still go on to the next grade.

At recess we played Multiplication Mambo. Each class got new CD roms called "There's Something About Decimals." After lunch we played Funny Phonics. Miss Malarkey said you never know what's going to be on THE TEST.

The closer we got to "THE TEST DAY," the weirder things got. When I brought the attendance sheets to the office, I heard Principal Wiggins yelling about pencils.

THIS IS THE TEST!
I want the good No. 2 pencils.
Not the kind with the crumbly erasers.
And I will personally make sure
they're all sharpened perfectly.
Pencil Report

The cafeteria lady, Mrs. Slopdown, took away the potato chips and served only fish.

In art we each made posters about THE TEST. Mrs. Magenta also showed us how to color in all those little circles they put on tests.

During gym we didn't play baseball or even exercise. Mr. Fittanuff said we had to prepare our minds and bodies for THE TEST. We all learned something about meditating and about something called "yogurt." Like I said, things were getting pretty weird at school. I got to thinking THE TEST was sort of important.

Your mind and body are one with **THE TEST.**

Even my mom knew about THE TEST. When she read me my bedtime story, I had to complete a ditto and give the main idea before I could go to sleep.

Mom started making me eat a really big breakfast. For lunch she packed me a Power Bar 2000. When I got to school, I traded Adam for a fat-free bran muffin. He traded with Hanna for a Baggie of carrot sticks. Hanna didn't want the Power Bar so she asked her best friend, Meredith, if she would trade for her apple. Somehow someone must have wanted the apple, and I'm not sure what happened but I had the Power Bar 2000 again.

One night Mom took me to a PTA meeting. A man was there talking about THE TEST. He wasn't a teacher or a parent or even the principal, but whoever he was he seemed to think THE TEST was very important. So did the parents.

The day of THE TEST the janitor, Mr. Surley, closed off the whole hallway. You couldn't even walk down it unless you had a pass. And you had to whisper. Miss Malarkey had to whisper the secret password to Mr. Surley before she could go to Room 10.

TESTERS ONLY

NO TALKING!!

IPTU -TESTING- -AREA-

BE PREPARED

DANGER

That morning there were more teachers than kids waiting for the nurse.

Miss Malarkey's job was to hand out the No. 2 pencils and the scratch paper. She looked like she didn't get enough sleep. Principal Wiggins was keeping the time. We couldn't even touch THE TEST until he waved the flag. When it was time to start, he waved the flag so hard, something happened to his hair.

THE TEST took forever.
It took two whole
days. My friend Carmine
got in trouble for not
using his scratch paper
the right way. I thought
his ninja warrior looked
pretty good, though.

Miss Malarkey caught Barry with his
baseball cards.

Morgan got a stomachache and had to go to the nurse. The hall monitor gave her such a hard time, she threw up right in the hall.

When Miss Malarkey said to erase all your pencil marks, Janet erased her whole test.

Principal Wiggins was in the room for a while, but he had a stomachache and had to go to the nurse. I hope he didn't throw up in the hall too.

After THE TEST everybody got prizes and had treats and we got extra recess. Even Steven, who fell asleep two times during THE TEST. Miss Malarkey looked wiped out, and she didn't even take THE TEST.

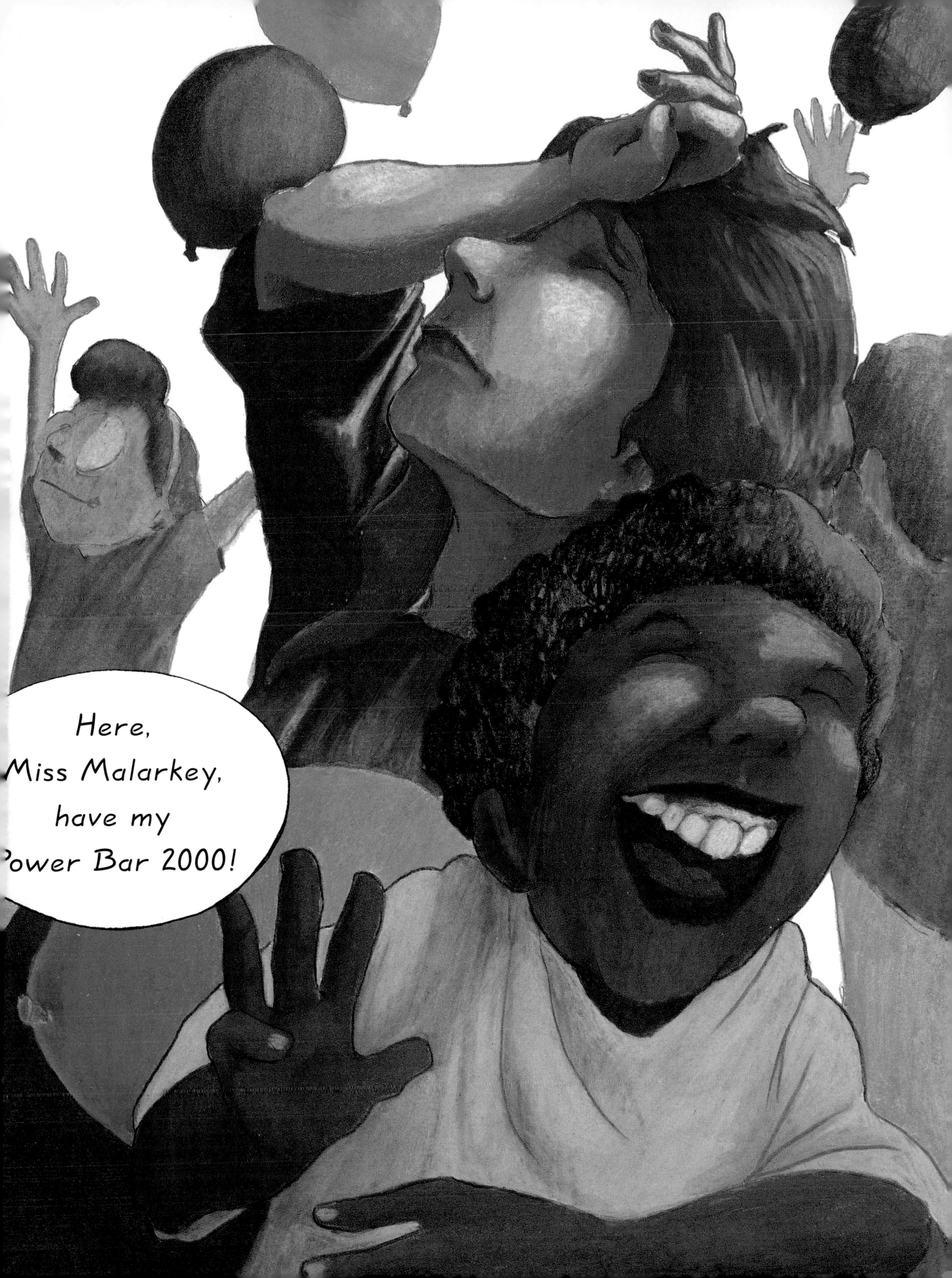
Here, Miss Malarkey, have my ower Bar 2000!

It's been a long time since we took THE TEST. Things are back to normal. Principal Wiggins isn't yelling quite as much. The cafeteria lady started serving potato chips again. Mom's packing me good old peanut butter and jelly sandwiches. And Miss Malarkey is letting her fingernails grow real long. I guess THE TEST really wasn't that important after all.